There's nothing Mr Toad likes more than a fast drive through the countryside. One day he trades his house, Toad Hall, for a fabulous new motor car. But Toad doesn't realise that the car is stolen — until the police accuse him of stealing it! Now Toad must come up with a daring plan to clear his name and get Toad Hall back...

British Library Cataloguing in Publication Data
Walt Disney's Mr Toad of Toad Hall.
813′.52[J]   PZ7
    ISBN 0-7214-1058-8

First edition

Printed in England

WALT DISNEY'S

Mr Toad
of Toad Hall

Ladybird Books

Down by a river, where the bulrushes
grow, there once stood a fine house.
The house belonged to young Mr Toad
and it was called Toad Hall.

Toad didn't know how to look after a
big house, so his friend McBadger took
care of it for him. Two more friends,
Rat and Mole, came visiting every day

But just lately, when Rat and Mole came calling, Toad was never at home. For Toad had a new craze! He had bought a caravan, and spent every day dashing all over the countryside with his horse, Cyril.

Although Toad went driving every day, he was no good at steering. Wherever he went, he left broken fences and smashed-up signposts. The houses he passed had shattered windows and churned-up lawns.

He had to pay for all the damage, but he didn't care. His caravan meant more to him than all the money in the world. But every day, more bills came pouring in.

"You can't afford to go on like this!"
cried McBadger.

Next day, he sent for Rat and Mole.
"Toad has no money left!" he told
them.

Rat and Mole were shocked, and sat
down with McBadger to think up a way
for Toad to make some money.

In the end, McBadger shook his head
and said, "There's only one thing for it.
Toad must sell Toad Hall!"

Suddenly, the door burst open and in came Toad, full of joy after his day out. McBadger told him the bad news. "You've no money left, Toad. You'll have to sell Toad Hall," he said.

Toad refused point blank. "Never!" he cried.

So McBadger, Rat and Mole marched
him upstairs and locked him in his
bedroom. There he must stay, they told
him, until he gave up the caravan and
paid his bills.

Toad lay upon his bed and sniffed.
A tear trickled down his cheek.

"It isn't *my* fault if things get in the way," Toad said to himself. "I don't *mean* to damage things."

But Toad soon grew bored with sulking. Suddenly he had an idea...

When darkness fell, Toad took the sheets off his bed and tied them into a rope. Then he gave a special whistle and, by the time he had shinned down the sheets, there was Cyril waiting for him.

"Where to?" neighed the horse. "The high road? The low road?"

"There's only one road for us!" cried Toad. "And that's the road to adventure!"

The Ugly Duck

Toad and Cyril set off with the caravan,
leaving their usual trail of destruction
behind them. By morning, Toad was
feeling distinctly peckish, so they
stopped at an inn.

14

But standing outside the inn was a
shining red motor car. In the twinkling
of an eye, Toad got over his craze for
caravans. Whatever the cost, he now
wanted that motor car.

Toad put on his biggest smile and swaggered into the inn.

A group of weasels sat drinking at one of the tables. They all glared at Toad.

"Hello there!" cried Toad. "Could anyone tell me who owns that motor car outside? I'd like to buy it!"

Instantly, the innkeeper and the weasels smiled and showed a lot of sharp teeth.

Never for a moment did Toad guess that the innkeeper, whose name was Mr Winkie, was the evil boss of the wicked Weasel Gang, or that the Weasel Gang were car thieves.

The motor car was stolen!

"The motor car is mine." said
Mr Winkie.

Toad took out his wallet. "I'm afraid I
don't have any money," he said. "But
I do have *this* – the title deed to my
house! You may know it. Biggish place,
down by the river..."

"Not *Toad Hall*!" breathed Winkie, snatching the deed from Toad's hand. They both signed it and Mr Winkie cried, "The motor car is yours!"

"And Toad Hall is yours!" answered Mr Toad, dashing to the door. "Hurrah!"

In a flash, Toad was in the driving seat of his new motor car. With a toot on his horn he shot off, leaving Cyril far behind.

Toad flashed past a policeman on a motorbike. Toad didn't notice him, but the policeman saw Toad's stolen car, all right! He raced after Toad, forcing him to stop.

"I'm arresting you!" snapped the policeman, jumping off his motorbike.

"Whatever for?" asked Toad.

"For stealing this motor car!" answered the policeman. Then, seizing Toad by the scruff of the neck, he hauled him off to the police station.

Next day, all the newspaper headlines said that Mr Toad had been arrested for stealing the motor car. McBadger, Rat and Mole were horrified.

"I don't believe a word of it," said Mole.

"Well," said McBadger with a sigh, "I know young Toad is always getting into trouble, but he's never stolen anything in his life!"

But someone *had* stolen the motor car, and Toad *had* been driving it. So if Toad wasn't guilty, who was? The three friends hadn't a clue.

*   *   *

Toad had to tell his story to a judge. He told him that he had bought the car from Mr Winkie in exchange for Toad Hall.

But Mr Winkie said that he knew nothing about Toad Hall or the motor car. Unfortunately for Toad, the judge believed Mr Winkie.

The judge glared at Toad and said,
"For committing this terrible crime, you
must be punished." And poor Toad was
sent to prison!

Toad was locked up all by himself. He
just sat on his little stool, staring at the
walls of his cell.

That evening, he was surprised to hear a
key turning in the door. In came the
jailer, and behind him was someone
whom Toad couldn't see very clearly.

"A visitor for you, Prisoner Toad,"
said the jailer. And in walked a
mysterious lady. The lady was wearing a
fur-trimmed coat and carrying a muff.
A long veil covered her face.

Toad couldn't think who the mysterious lady might be.

As soon as the jailer had gone, she whipped the veil away from her face.

"Goodness!" thought Toad. "She's got a face like a horse!"

And then a wide grin spread across Toad's face. For the mysterious lady was none other than his old friend and partner in adventure, Cyril the horse!

Cyril had worked out a plan for Toad's escape. Inside the muff he had hidden a pink frock and a grey bonnet.

Toad put the clothes on. "No one will ever guess it's you, Mr Toad," Cyril said. "All you have to do is to slip out when you get the chance. They'll think you're the washerwoman."

Toad hated the idea, but he agreed to give it a try. Cyril replaced his veil and the jailer came to let him out. "Good luck," Cyril whispered as he left.

Later that night Toad was free!

Toad walked and walked, wondering where to go. In the end, he decided to try Rat's house.

Rat and Mole were sitting in front of a roaring fire, clutching mugs of steaming cocoa. They almost jumped out of their skins when a little old washerwoman tumbled into the room. But they would have known that voice anywhere!

"I didn't steal anything!" it wailed.
"I'm innocent!"

Toad soon felt better after a mug of cocoa. Just as he was telling Rat and Mole all about his escape, McBadger arrived. He had discovered that Mr Winkie and the Weasel Gang were living in Toad Hall.

Something had to be done about it! So
late that night they put on their hats,
got into a rowing boat and headed
up-river towards Toad Hall. Weasels or
no weasels, they were determined to
prove that Toad was not guilty!

Toad and his friends rowed as fast as they could towards a cavern in the river bank. It led to a secret flight of steps going up through the cellars of Toad Hall. Up and up they crept, but no one saw them.

At last they reached a gallery that overlooked the living room.

On a sofa below them, fast asleep, lay
Mr Winkie. And poking out of his
jacket pocket was the very thing they
were after: the title deed to Toad Hall!

Remembering how Toad had escaped
from his bedroom, Rat slipped away to
fetch some sheets to make into a rope.
They tied Mole (who was the lightest) to
one end, then lowered him down until
he was hovering above the sleeping
Mr Winkie.

Cautiously, Mole reached down and
tweaked the title deed from Winkie's
pocket. In triumph, the others hauled
him to safety.

They fled from Toad Hall and showed
the deed to the police. There was
Winkie's signature! It proved that
Winkie had been telling lies and Toad
had been telling the truth all along.

So the police raided Toad Hall and
captured Winkie and the weasels. Next
day, there were more headlines in the
newspapers about Toad. But this time
they all said, "Not Guilty!"

A few days later, McBadger sat with Rat and Mole in the living room of Toad Hall. "Well," said McBadger, "Toad has mended his ways. No more caravans! No more motor cars! No more crazes!"

Suddenly there was a crash and pieces of chimney came tumbling down. Swooping overhead was an aeroplane. And the pilot was Toad!

"Hello there!" Toad shouted gaily.
"Wonderful things, these planes."

Toad had got a new craze after all.
Dear, lovable Toad would never mend
his ways.